Hodder Toddler

....

For Joshua and his grandparents:
Sondra and Mayo Simon
Gwen and Hugh Stamp
F.S.

For Tanja
D.M.

A catalogue record of this book is available from the British Library.

ISBN 0 340 79212 4 PB

Text copyright © Francesca Simon 1996
Illustrations copyright © David Melling 1996
Designed by Rowan Seymour

First edition published 1996
by Hodder Children's Books
a division of Hodder Headline Limited
338 Euston Road London NW1 3BH

This edition published 2001

10 9 8

Printed in China

What's That Noise?

Francesca Simon • David Melling

Hodder
Children's
Books

A division of Hodder Headline Limited

One night Harry went to sleep at
Grandpa and Grandma's house.

For the first time in his life,
Harry *slept* in a strange bed,
in a strange room.

It was very dark.

Suddenly Harry heard a strange noise.

SPUTTER-CLICK SPUTTER-CLICK
WHOOOSH!

"Grandpa, Grandpa, come quickly!" shouted Harry. "What's that noise?"

Grandpa ran upstairs to Harry's room.

No noise here.

No noise there.

No noise anywhere.

Then suddenly . . .

"Harry, it's only the radiator.
Now snuggle down and go to sleep."

Everything was quiet until . . .

NEE NAW NEE NAW

"Grandpa, Grandpa, come quickly!
What's that noise?"

"Harry, it's only . . .

Now snuggle down and go to sleep."

Everything was quiet again until . . .

RUMBLE RUMBLE **RUMBLE**

"Grandpa, Grandpa, come quickly!
What's that noise?"

"Harry, it's only . . .

an aeroplane.

RUMBLE RUMBLE VR

OOM!

Now snuggle down and go to sleep."

Everything was quiet until . . .

RAT-TAT RAT-TAT RAT-TAT-TAT

"Grandpa, Grandpa, come quickly!
What's that noise?"

"Harry, it's only . . .

Mrs Ruffle next door
hammering.

RAT-TAT RAT-TAT RAT-TAT-TAT

"Now snuggle down and go to sleep."

For a while everything was quiet.
Grandpa settled down in his comfy bed
and read his book.

Suddenly he heard a strange snuffling noise.

snuffle   snuffle

"Grandma, Grandma, come quickly!
What's that noise?"

"I don't know," said Grandma.

They heard the snuffling rustling again,
only this time it was louder.

snuffle

snuffle

"I think the noise is coming from Harry's room," whispered Grandma.

Grandma and Grandpa
tiptoed up the stairs
to the attic.

The snuffling noise
got closer . . .

and closer...

Slowly Grandma opened
Harry's door.

Now snuggle down and go to sleep."

Goodbye
Hodder Toddler